“Have you seen any butterflies today?” Billy asked his friend, Molly Mouse. “No,” said Molly. “But there might be one hiding in the primrose patch. Let’s look.”